Travel to Maurice's World!

Let your passport to adventure take you to Maurice's imaginary world online, beginning with Maurice's Secret Sycamore Tree app.

Additional apps take you inside each book in the *Maurice's Valises* series. Spend time in the playroom. Make friends and learn things from all over the world. Play fun games, earn mouse coins and moral badges, and collect your treasures in your own online valise. Use the special code below to begin. And even more activities are to come soon!

YOUR SPECIAL CODE IS **PREPARE**

The Books Before...

In the Beginning

In the first book, Maurice, an orphan mouse, travels to New Zealand, where he is visited by the Muse of Mice and is given a great responsibility. Maurice learns the value of always telling the truth.

The Micetro of Moscow

In the second book, Maurice travels to Russia, where he befriends a musical (yet unpopular) mouse, Henry, who helps Tchaikovsky finish *Swan Lake*. Maurice learns that everyone is special in his or her own way.

Casablanca

In the third book, Maurice's adventures take him to Morocco, where a selfless act helps a bespectacled camel, Cecil, and Maurice learns the true meaning of friendship.

Medicine Mouse

In the fourth book, Maurice journeys to America. Traveling west, he befriends a kindly prairie dog, Pip, and meets a Medicine Mouse who shares his life's wisdom with Maurice.

Kookoo Mountain

In the fifth book, Maurice journeys to a hidden Alpine valley, where he meets Oswyn, a wise old owl, and learns a life lesson of questioning from this experience.

A Christmas Tail

In the sixth book, Maurice travels to Bavaria, where he encounters a circus elephant and an anteater, and he experiences the joy of giving to others.

The Books Before...

The Muuha of Bang Bua
In Maurice's seventh story, he survives an ocean voyage and a monsoon, and he reaches his journey's end on a sandbar in the middle of a river in Thailand. Maurice encounters the revered teacher Muuha and learns another important lesson of life.

The Beans of Budapest
In Maurice's eighth adventure, he finds himself becoming part of a gypsy family, where he learns the value and joy of teaching others.

Museum Mouse
Museum Mouse is the ninth book in the series, in which Maurice finds himself exploring the Egyptian Museum in Cairo, where he meets his Muse and learns about her darker side, the Muddler, and the real treasure of the Moral Scroll.

"It's best to prepare today for what might happen tomorrow."

—*Aesop*

Foreword

Imagine you're walking in an open field of yellow and red wildflowers on a sunny day. You look down and see several adorable brown bunnies, huddled together. Suddenly, the bunnies rise from the ground, forming a circle over your head, spinning clockwise. They begin to sing the "Happy Birthday" song to you.

A strange vision ... and a magical one. Not that the scene itself is magical, but rather the fact that I wrote it, you read it, and then it appeared in your own mind. Images that began in my brain ended up in yours. Legerdemain!

That's the enchantment of reading. An eager reader opens a book and willingly allows the carefully crafted thoughts of another human being to enter his or her own. Thoughts become moments played out through the subjective lens of each individual's personal experiences. And then ... the miracle. Those moments become memories, a mental cousin to our nocturnal dreams, and meld to the reader's psyche as would any genuine, real-life experience.

This writer-to-reader intimacy can be impactful in a way that television and movies rarely are. A powerful book can provoke a deep reconsideration of one's life path, alter a reader's perception of long-held beliefs, and trigger a menu of emotions that bear a soulful heft not usually associated with spoon-fed media.

Read a book and mingle with the Grand Vizier of the Ottoman Empire, or negotiate the Mississippi via rickety raft with Huck and Tom. Feel the heat of a volcano or the blistering Arctic freeze. Cry and laugh and marvel and wonder at amazing the sights of Earth and beyond. All thanks to the carefully crafted words on a blank sheet of paper.

Imagine that.

— *Mark Valenti*

Mark Valenti is an acclaimed American writer, known for his work in both television and film.

ISBN: 978-94-91613-14-2-51695

MOUSE PRINTS PRESS
Prinsengracht 1053-S Boot
1017 JE Amsterdam Netherlands

Maurice's Valises

Valises

Moral Tails in an
Immoral World

Foreword by Mark Valenti

Kansas and the Crow

By J. S. Friedman
Illustrations by Chris Beatrice

As the last of the little group of mice returned on this moonlit night with more twigs for his already tall twig-pile, Grandpa Maurice threw all his weight against the front door and pushed until it clicked closed.

But he wasn't fast enough. Some icy winds whisked in too.

To make matters worse, the uninvited wintry winds went around the room bothering everyone.

All the grandmice *(98, to be exact)*, plus some forest friends, plus Maurice, had to rub their front paws together in order to warm up.

This didn't stop—not until more twigs were added to the fire in the fireplace.

Then the fire roared, rewarming the living room—deep in the woods, in the base of an old sycamore tree.

Now the winter's winds could only worry what they could outside.

Maurice checked his special storytelling chair to see if it felt toasty and to make sure no windy worries were waiting on his seat.

It did. And there weren't.

So he sat.

"Call me Maurice," said Grandpa Maurice, smiling.
He continued, "Tonight is a good night for the story
of Kansas and the Crow."

So Maurice stood and turned to the towering stack of
old valises behind him.

Each was covered with stickers from a place
Maurice had taken it to.

Maurice looked for the old,
rumpled valise marked "Kansas."

He pulled it from the stack.

Dusted it off.

Undid the old, tattered
buckle straps.

And opened it, and guess
what?

Moths flew out!

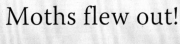

Out of respect for the moths, Maurice waited until they fluttered away. Then he pulled out some old corncobs; an old, tattered *(and a little moth-eaten)* hobo hat; overalls; and a farm shirt.

And last, but not least, he pulled out a rolled-up Moral Scroll.

"Well," said Maurice, resettling into his chair with his storytelling muffler around his neck and his hobo hat atop his head, "this is a story that you should pass on to your children—when you are old enough to have children, and when they're old enough to understand you."

PAW NOTE

 A hobo is a wandering person looking for work and food.

PAW NOTE

A Moral Scroll is a paper with a wise saying written on it. The saying is the lesson learned from a particular traveling tale.

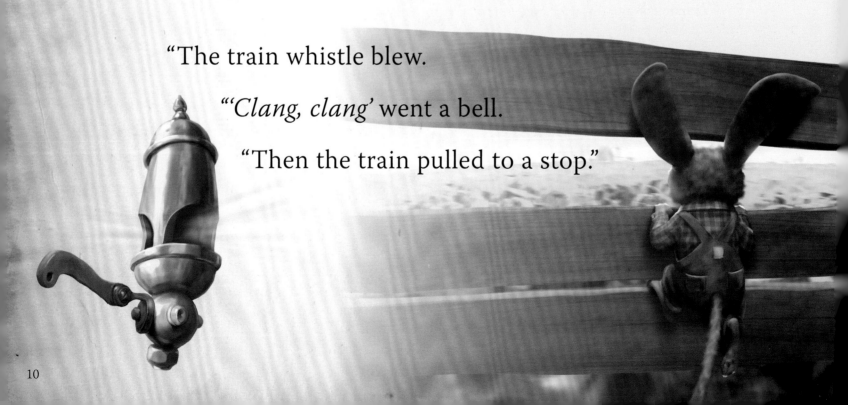

"Many, many years ago, I found myself traveling on a freight train across America.

"Days went by, yet the landscape never changed. Whenever I looked out through a crack in the wall of the rail car, all I saw were cornfields stretching out to where they met the sky.

"Just as I was getting thirsty and had gone through my stash of food, the train began to slow.

"The train whistle blew.

"'*Clang, clang*' went a bell.

"Then the train pulled to a stop."

"I peered through the crack and saw a small town in the middle of—guess what?"

"More cornfields?" cried 98 little voices.

"Right! And men started shouting and tugging open the doors to the freight cars.

"I gathered my things into my valise and then hung my valise from my walking stick.

"When the train doors rattled open, I jumped to the ground and hid behind a big, iron train wheel.

"And it didn't take long for the train whistle to blow again.

"Then the doors of the freight car rattled shut again, and off chugged the train.

"And I ran for the fields."

"Surrounded by stalks of green, I was lost in a forest of corn. I got scared. I didn't know which way to go.

"But suddenly, there it was: the voice of the Muse of Mice, my protector, who gently whispered, 'Maurice, go forward—your path will be revealed. Believe, and you will find it.'

"I stumbled forward through the cornstalks, and then, there it was—a path. So I followed it, trudging along, lugging this very valise over my shoulder, where it dangled from my walking stick."

PAW NOTE

The Muse of Mice has been the spiritual protector and guide of Maurice since his birth.

"Eventually, I reached a clearing. There, an old willow tree was bent so low that its branches reached into a welcoming little pond. Tall grasses gave the pond plenty of privacy."

14

"At one edge lay a perfectly round patch of little green plants, their small shoots and yellow flowers stretching out along the ground, growing every which way. So I drank some cool pond water, then lay down under the welcoming willow tree for a nap."

15

"I awoke to a rain of yellow things falling on my head. I heard *'Caw, caw.'* I looked up and saw a black crow lying on a branch overhead.

"'What are you doing way out here?' said the bird. 'Come to pick an early pumpkin?' he asked jokingly, balancing on his back, holding a corncob with his feet and pecking the kernels.

"'I just awoke from a sound sleep, thank you very much,' I replied. 'I'm Maurice—who might you be?'"

"'Chester's the name, carefree is the game,' said the crow, spitting more kernels into the air. 'I live in this wonderful tree, without a worry in the world.'

"Chester liked talking, so I heard his stories about Kansas *(which, it turns out, was where we were)*. He gossiped about the locals, like Lilac the Skunk; Gretchen the Groundhog and Piggyback Pete, her companion; the time-telling swallow Sonja; Indus the Beaver; and Hilton the Hawk. He also told me about the pumpkin patch on the other side of the pond."

17

"As the sun lowered in the sky, and swallows swooped for their dinner of bugs, my stomach told me it was my dinnertime too. I told Chester that I had to look for food.

"'Not to worry, Maurice,' said Chester, as he spit another kernel into the air. 'There's always lots of corn on the ground, and soon there will be pumpkins over there in the not-so-hidden pumpkin patch.

"'Of course, you have to watch out for Hilton the Hawk—he'd love to meet you in the open fields,' he warned.

"Even so, I went off looking for food—but every once in a while, I made sure to peek up at the sky for Hilton."

"Just past the clearing was a field with corn lying everywhere. I dashed over and got enough for my daily meal, but I also filled my valise—just in case.

"Above me, squeaking swarms of swallows swooped low over the fields and pond, scooping their suppers.

"As night got closer, I looked for shelter at the base of the willow tree. There I found a large, round hole leading to an abandoned den that had once belonged to Gretchen the Groundhog, who seemed to have moved.

"I crawled in.

"I looked around."

"And I thought, well, maybe with a few improvements,
I could set up home for the winter.

"So I grabbed some twigs and blades of grass and
dragged them in to make a bed."

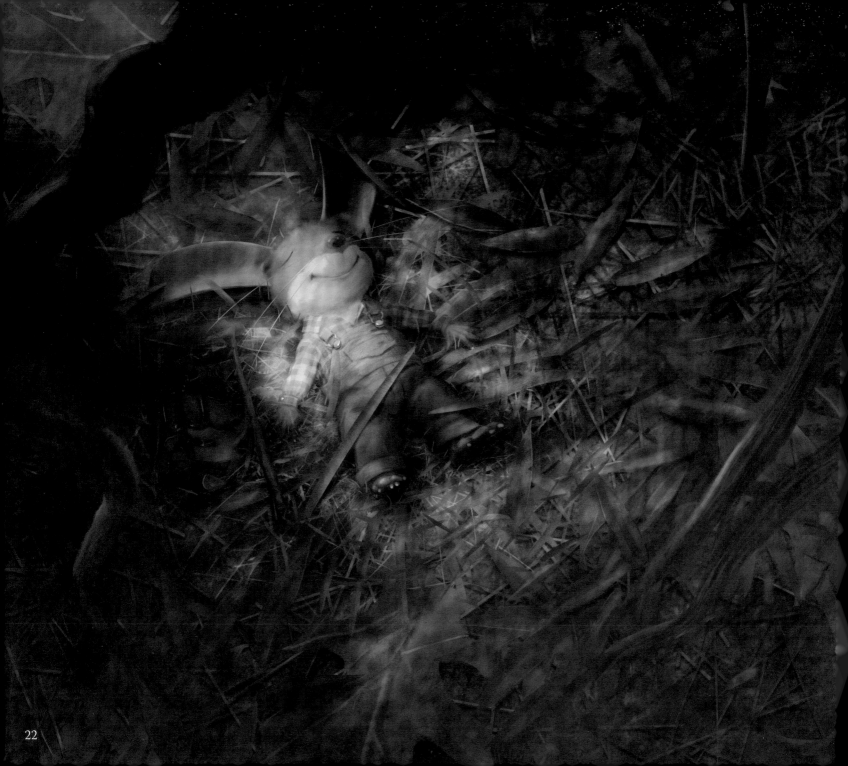

"Above me, I could still hear Chester: 'What's the rush, mouse? Caw ... plenty of time, caw, caw. Relax there, Mr. Maurice, caw, caw, caw.'

"I didn't know it then, but I was to hear that caw caw cawing for a very long time, day in and week out, from that cawing crow.

"I worked till moonrise. Then I pulled my things into my new home and snuggled into my new bed to sleep.

"And Chester was still cawing on his branch above.

"A few days later, I was by the pond, looking for wood to make furniture for my home.

"But I found more than wood. I came face to face with a skunk drinking water.

"Startled, she pulled up her head and stared at me.

"'Whowhowhoooo are you?' she stuttered. Her tail shot up into the air—she was ready to spray me with that nasty smell skunks have."

"'I'm Maurice. You must be Lilac.'

"'No one ever tttttttalks to me! They run away from me, yelling *stttinky Lilac*,' she sniffled.

"'Well, not me,' I said and kept gathering wood.

"Lilac looked surprised.

"Then she relaxed.

"Down came her tail. *(Thank goodness!)*

"And she went back to slurping from the pond.

"When she'd had her fill, she said, 'Wwwwwelcome to the neighborhood—see you again,' and she wandered off, waving good-bye with her swishing tail.

"A splash in the pond created a ring of ripples. There was a perfect pile of sticks floating a short distance from the water's edge.

"Suddenly, a head bobbed up from the water, and a beaver with a branch in his mouth swam to the pile."

"Back and forth, forth and back went the busy beaver, once in a while stopping, circling, and waving.

"Weeks passed like this, and life on the prairie became a mixture of gathering food to store for later and listening to Chester splash in the pond or babble from his favorite branch.

"Unfortunately, when Chester decided to take a nap, his steady *kicaaaw ... kicaaaw ... kicaaaw* snores would keep me from my nap. The difference was, I was tired from doing work. He was tired from doing no work.

"One day, I met Gretchen the Groundhog. As I lay lazily reading a book by the pond, there came a sudden dust storm, or so I thought—but actually, dirt was raining from Gretchen, who had Piggyback Pete harnessed on her back. She was busy kicking and digging a new hole in the ground.

"'Oh, pardon me,' said Gretchen, once she realized she had showered me."

"'Never too early to dig a new entrance to my home by the pumpkin patch—location, location, location, I always say. They're looking mighty ripe, you know,' and she went back to burrowing.

"'Excuse me,' I said, 'but why is the little fellow on your back?'

"'Well,' said Gretchen, stopping her digging, 'there was a tunnel cave-in when Pete was born, and his back legs don't work. And he lost his parents too, so I've kind of carried him ever since. That's why I keep moving houses. He keeps growing.'"

"Finally fall found its cooler days and colder nights at the welcoming pond.

"It also found me by the pond's edge, with a string hanging off a pole and into the water.

"Chester came by and cawed, 'What are you doing, and what's that sign on your door, *Gone Friending?*'

"'I'm friending.'

"'You're what?' cawed Chester.

"'I tie food to the string and feed frogs. Then we become friends.'

"'Caw-mical,' said Chester, chuckling."

"And then came swallow time, when fall's setting sun went down each day a little earlier, signaling the flock to feed on fewer flying bugs.

"The swallows realized the days were getting shorter. It was time to begin their long, yearly journey to follow the sun.

"Sonja, the lead swallow, swooped her last swoop and gathered her flock, and together they flew south to South America for the winter.

"One cooling but lazy afternoon, days later, I said to Chester, 'Don't you think you should gather some corn and pumpkin seeds for the coming winter?'

"'Not to worry, Maurice—there's plenty of food on the ground. Look, pumpkins are ripe for the picking. Calm yourself. You spend too much time working. Not enough time relaxing.'"

"One morning, not a month later, I woke to an unusual stillness.

"I rolled out of bed and peeked outside, where a thick blanket of fresh white snow covered the ground. Then I went back under the covers to sleep.

"I was dreaming about my Muse and her Muddler quarreling about kindness, when I heard, 'Caw, caw, Maurice, are you awake?'

"I got up again and stuck my nose out of my doorway.

"There, huddled at my entrance, stood Chester, covered in snow, shivering.

"'Maurice, do you have something to eat? I can't find corn on the ground, the pumpkins are mostly harvested, and it's snowing again.'

"I went to my storeroom—which Gretchen had dug, and that I had stocked all summer and fall—and gave Chester some corn and pumpkin seeds."

"The next morning Chester was back, this time covered with a thick coat of snow and ice.

"'Mmmauuuuriiice,' he shivered, 'my beak is nearly frozen. Can I have some more food? I can't find corn on the ground with all this new snow.'

"Again, I gave him some corn and pumpkin seeds from my storeroom.

"This went on for days. Finally, Chester moved in—or, really, part of him moved in."

"He could barely fit. He backed in and sat quietly, crammed into the doorway, peering out and waiting for the snow to stop.

"It took days, or maybe a week—though it felt like years—but finally, the snow stopped.

"The world was all white and quiet outside *(except for Chester)*. He didn't know what to do. His tail feathers were warm inside, but his head wore a little icecap outside, since he was still wedged into the doorway of the den."

"He knew he couldn't find food.

"He knew he had no proper nest for winter.

"And at last he cawed, 'Maurice, I have to fly south to find my family flock—to get away from this cold and find food and shelter.

"'I laughed at your preparations all summer and fall.

"'Now I know: all play and no work makes Chester a cold and hungry crow.

"'I can't thank you enough for helping me survive.'

"Both grateful and embarrassed, Chester shook the ice off his head and took to the air.

"He made a small circle in the sky, and then off he flew (*nonstop*) to Miami.

"The end."

There was a silence in the room. Then, curiosity got the better of the den.

"Grandpa Maurice, was the moral of the story location, location, location—to live where it's warm, so there's plenty of food, like in Miami?" asked Minierva, grandmouse number 55.

"Let's see," said Maurice as he unrolled the roll of the Moral Scroll.

He turned the old paper for all to see as he read,

It's best to
prepare today
for what might
happen tomorrow

"It's best to prepare today for what might happen tomorrow."

Minierva looked surprised.

But the grandmice who had been sent out for more twigs to add to the already-tall twig-pile weren't surprised. They understood.

Good thing, too. Because Maurice's eyes had closed, and as usual after a good nighttime story, he was already snoring. And his steady *kicaaaw ... kicaaaw ... kicaaaw* snores sounded just like someone else's we know.

The end, again.
(But more to come ...)

Backword

Aesop, a slave and storyteller, is thought to have lived in ancient Greece between 620 and 560 BCE. He may not have solely composed the fables history has attributed to him. No writings by Aesop remain, but numerous fables credited to him were gathered across the centuries and in many languages in a storytelling tradition that continues to this day. Animals, insects, and inanimate objects that speak, solve problems, and generally reflect a wide range of human characteristics characterized most of these allegorical tales.

Mark Valenti is a seasoned American writer/producer best known for family-oriented television programs. He began his career as a production associate at Steven Spielberg's Amblin Entertainment and has achieved international distinction writing for such companies as Showtime, ABC Family Channel, Disney, Paramount, Twentieth Century Fox, and DreamWorks.

map of
Maurice's
Travels

Questions to Chew On

The grandmice "had to rub their front paws together in order to warm up." Have you ever done that? When? Why? How does it work?

Maurice's valises are covered with stickers from places he has visited. What would your valise look like? Draw a few stickers to put on your valise, and share your travels with a classmate.

Why do moths fly out of old, dark valises? Are there places in your house you may find some moths?

Maurice told the children they should pass the story on to their children when they were old enough to understand it. How old would that be? Why?

Maurice saw cornfields stretching out to "where they met the sky." What do we call that faraway place? Have you ever seen it? What do you call it? Does it change in its appearance?

What did the Muse of Mice mean when she told Maurice to "go forward—your path will be revealed. Believe, and you will find it"? Believe, and you will find it?" Have you ever believed in something so hard that it happened? What?

What do you think of the names of the locals? Lilac the Skunk, Gretchen the Groundhog, Piggyback Pete, Chester.

Why did the author choose those names? Why have you chosen a name for a pet of yours or for a character in a story you wrote?

Maurice filled his valise with corn "just in case." Have you ever done anything "just in case"? What and why?

Why did Lilac's tail come down after Maurice talked to her? Why do you think she speaks with a stutter?

Maurice's sign said 'Gone Friending." What would you do to attract a new friend?

Why did Maurice give Chester his corn and pumpkin seeds? Why did he have enough to share when Chester had so little?

How do people prepare for blizzards or bad storms?

What did Chester mean by "All play and no work makes Chester a cold and hungry crow"? Have you ever heard a saying that is similar to that? What did it mean?

The moral of this story is "It's best to prepare today for what might happen tomorrow." When have you forgotten to prepare and wished you had?

Acknowledgments

I wish to acknowledge, as I have through this series, my ever-growing list of helpers, without whom I could not publish this book.

My special thanks, as always to Elías R. Ragnarsson in Reykjavik, my time zone traveler and colleague, for his diligence and patience in working strange hours both in the day and night.

Many thanks to Stephanie Arnold for her early editorial contributions and to Renee Rooks Cooley for her constant copyediting expertise.

To Paula Prentiss for her educational questions and to Marion Pothoff in Amsterdam for her expert eye in pre-press.

To my wife, Cheryl, thank you for your tolerance in sharing our lives with this mouse.

And, as always, my many thanks to my coconspirator of imagination, Chris Beatrice, whose illustrative artistry transforms my thoughts into, as someone said, a banquet for the eyes, a meal for the mind.